WHITNEY COACHES DAVID ON FIGHTING GOLIATH

and learns to stand up for herself

THE EMERALD BIBLE
COLLECTION

THERESE JOHNSON BORCHARD
ILLUSTRATIONS BY WENDY VANNEST

PAULIST PRESS
NEW YORK / MAHWAH, N.J.

Library of Congress Cataloging-in-Publication Data

Borchard, Therese Johnson.
    Whitney coaches David on fighting Goliath : and learns to stand up for herself / by Therese Johnson Borchard ; illustrations by Wendy VanNest.
        p. cm. — (The Emerald Bible Collection)
    Summary : Having been transported by her emerald Bible back to the time of David, ten-year-old Whitney helps him fight the giant Goliath and thus gains the courage to confront an intimidating girl at school.
    ISBN 0-8091-6669-0 (alk. paper)
    1. David, King of Israel—Juvenile fiction. 2. Goliath, (Biblical giant)—Juvenile fiction. [1. David, King of Israel— Fiction. 2. Goliath (Biblical giant)—Fiction. 3. Courage— Fiction. 4. Conduct of life—Fiction. 5. Time travel—Fiction.] I. VanNest, Wendy, ill. II. Title. III. Series.

PZ7.B64775 Wd 1999
[Fic]—dc21   99–042615
                                                                                   CIP

Published by Paulist Press
997 Macarthur Boulevard
Mahwah, New Jersey 07430

www.paulistpress.com

Printed and bound in the United States of America

The Emerald Bible Collection
is dedicated
to the loving memory of
Whitney Bickham Johnson

TABLE OF CONTENTS

NANA'S EMERALD BIBLE

It was a warm August morning the day the Bickham family moved from their Michigan home to a residence in a western suburb of Chicago. Mr. Bickham's mother, Nana, who had lived with the family for some time, had passed away in February of that same year. Not long after, Mr. Bickham landed a great new job; however, it meant the whole family would have to leave everything that was familiar to them in Michigan and start again in Chicago.

It was especially hard on Whitney and Howard, the two Bickham children. They had grown accustomed to their school in Michigan and had several friends there. They didn't want to have to start over at a new school. Whitney, especially, was heartbroken about moving away from Michigan, for Nana's death alone had been very difficult on her. For Whitney, the Bickhams' Michigan home was filled with wonderful memories of Nana that she did not want to leave behind.

Nana and Whitney had had a very special friendship. Since Mrs. Bickham worked a day job that kept her very busy, it was Nana that had cared for Whitney from the time she was a baby. Growing up, Whitney spent endless hours with Nana. Her most wonderful memories of Nana centered around those afternoons when the two would go down to the basement and read stories from the Bible. Nana would sit on her favorite chair and read a story to

Whitney that related in some way to a problem Whitney was having. As Whitney sat on her grandma's lap listening to the story, her own situation always became a little clearer.

When Nana became sick and knew she was going to die, she called Whitney into her room and said:

"Dear Whitney, you know how special you are to me. I want you to have something that will always bring you home to me. I have a favorite possession that I'd like to leave with you—my Emerald Bible. Every time you open this special book, you will find yourself in another world—at a place far away from your own, and in a time way before your birth. But I will be right there with you."

Nana was so weak that she could barely go on, but, knowing the importance of her message, she pushed herself to say these last words:

"Whatever you do in the years

ahead, keep this Bible with you, as it will help you with all of life's most difficult lessons. And remember, when you open its pages, I am there with you."

As Nana closed her eyes to enter into an eternal sleep, Whitney spotted the beautiful Emerald Bible that lay at Nana's side. It sparkled like a massive jewel, and on its cover were engraved the words, "Lessons of Life."

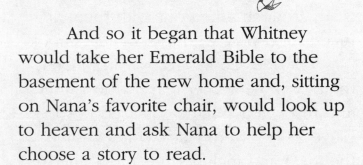

And so it began that Whitney would take her Emerald Bible to the basement of the new home and, sitting on Nana's favorite chair, would look up to heaven and ask Nana to help her choose a story to read.

CHAPTER ONE

THE CLIQUE

Although Whitney missed her old friends back in Michigan, she was beginning to feel accepted by the crowd at the new school. Her immediate group of friends—Le Ly, Tonya, and Maria—made her feel a part of their group, inviting her to sit with them at lunch, hang out with them at recess, and play with them after school.

Besides Le Ly, Tonya, and Maria, there was the soccer team, who valued and respected Whitney as a good soccer player. They were glad Whitney joined the team and included her in all the fun at practice and afterward.

There was one group of girls, however, that didn't particularly like Whitney. And that group happened to be the most popular clique of girls. They were the ones who organized after-school activities and slumber parties during the weekends. Anyone who got invited to one of their parties was "someone"; that person had made it "in." The popular group had the power to "make or break" a person, or so they thought.

There were three girls in particular who did not like Whitney: Nicki, Mary Jo, and Kim. They felt as though Whitney had been accepted too easily by everyone. And they were especially bothered by Whitney's friendship with two popular boys—Joe and Mike. Whitney had no interest in Joe or Mike except to be their friend. However, the fact that Joe and Mike enjoyed hanging out and playing soccer with Whitney was threatening to the three girls.

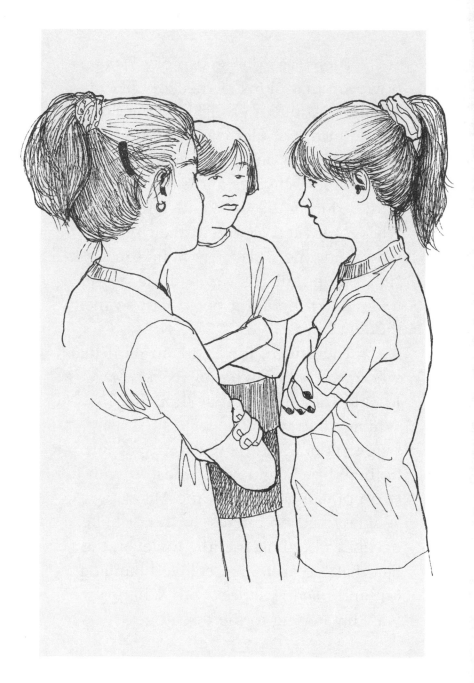

Nicki, Mary Jo, and Kim told the others that under no circumstances would Whitney be invited to the next slumber party. A little reserved about Whitney themselves, the other members of the clique agreed.

A couple of weeks later, Kim planned a large slumber party in celebration of her eleventh birthday. She asked her mom if she could invite twenty-five people, and her mom agreed. It was the biggest slumber party yet. Word had gotten out, and all the girls at school knew about it. Everyone anxiously awaited their invitations in the mail.

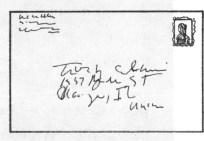

In Whitney's fifth-grade world, getting invited to Kim's party was comparable to being asked to attend the royal ball in the world of Cinderella. It was a stamp of approval—artificial, but meaningful, nonetheless.

Two weeks before the party, Tonya, Maria, and Le Ly showed up for soccer practice all excited.

"Did you get yours?" they asked one another, not having to explain what arrived in the mail. One at a time they nodded affirmatively.

Each of them was wearing a silly grin on her face when Whitney arrived.

"What's up with the goofy expression on everyone's face?" Whitney asked.

"Uh, well . . . ," Maria stuttered, not knowing whether to tell Whitney about the invitations or not.

"Each of us received an invitation to Kim's slumber party," Tonya stated so matter-of-factly that it took everyone off guard.

"Oh," Whitney replied. "That's great." She was trying to hide her

disappointment. "Why didn't mine arrive, too?" she wondered. Then she realized that no one had her new address. "That's it! That's gotta be it! How would they know where to send it?" She convinced herself this was the reason.

Whitney was sure she would be invited if Le Ly, Tonya, and Maria had been. After all, she felt pretty well accepted by everyone. She was even friends with Joe and Mike, the two popular boys. "Surely if Joe and Mike consider me a friend Kim will invite me," she thought to herself.

Whitney didn't think any more about Kim's party until the Thursday before the sleepover.

"Only two more days till the party," she told herself. "If I don't get an invitation by tomorrow, I guess I wasn't invited after all." It was starting to sink in, and she began to feel depressed. "I can't stand this not-knowing. There has got to be a way to find out if I am on the list, and if not, why."

The next day at recess Whitney asked Le Ly, Maria, and Tonya to find out if she was invited.

"Just ask Kim who all is coming. Don't bring up my name. Tell her you were curious to know who all was invited," Whitney explained to the group.

Everyone assigned Tonya to do the investigation. "Remember, Tonya," Whitney reminded her, "don't mention my name."

"OK, OK," Tonya said as she made her way over to the corner of the school parking lot, where the popular clique always mingled at recess.

"Hey, Kim," Tonya began, trying to be as cool and casual as she knew how. "I was just wondering . . . who all is going tomorrow night?" Tonya was

THE EMERALD BIBLE COLLECTION

relieved that it was out. She and her friends—and nearly every girl at the school—were intimidated by Kim, Mary Jo, Nicki, and the others. Approaching their corner at recess took courage.

"Ummm. Let's see . . . there's you, Maria, and Le Ly. There's the girls in my dance class. There's Audrey, Karen, Angie, and Sue. And then . . . ," Kim continued on and on, listing everyone Tonya knew or had heard of, even very shy girls in her class that weren't invited to anything.

"The only one I can think of that I didn't invite is Whitney," Kim said sort of maliciously.

Tonya was shocked. "Why in the world would she single out Whitney like that?" she wondered. She didn't know whether she should inquire any further, or just leave it alone. Before she had made up her mind, Kim blurted out the reason.

"I don't like Whitney. . . . She's weird. She wears all those strange outfits that were in fashion two years ago. She talks with an accent from the farmlands of Michigan. And she is too friendly with Mike and Joe."

Tonya froze, not knowing what to do. On the one hand, she liked Whitney and felt as though she should stick up for her. But, on the other hand, she didn't want to become next on Kim's list. For once, Tonya felt included by the clique. She was flattered to be invited to the party, and she didn't want to mess it up.

Tonya looked down, just thinking. "What should I do with all this information? What should I tell Whitney? Should I sugarcoat it? Or should I tell her flat out what Kim said?" Tonya wished that she could trade places with Le Ly or Maria. Why did she get this job anyway?

She avoided looking at Kim until

she knew what to say. But Kim continued before Tonya had a chance to get a word in. Kim was able to read Tonya's thoughts.

"You can tell Whitney I said all this. It is about time someone put her in her place."

With those hurtful words, Tonya left the circle of popular girls and returned to her set of friends. Her stomach was so knotted that it felt like a soccer scrimmage was taking place inside her. She could feel the sandwich she ate at lunch doing somersaults in the air.

Whitney, Le Ly, and Maria took one look at Tonya coming their way and ran to her aid.

"Oh my gosh," Maria said, "you look like you are about to get sick. Your face is so pale."

"Yeah, you don't look good, Tonya. If the expression on your face has anything to do with what happened

over there, I feel sorry for Whitney," Le Ly chimed in.

Whitney was silent. Tears welled up in her eyes. She knew immediately that she had not been invited intentionally, and that Kim had said some mean things about her.

For a while, Le Ly and Maria tended to Tonya, not noticing the tears that were now dripping down Whitney's face.

One question was all Whitney needed to ask Tonya to be sure. "It wasn't good, was it?" she asked as she wiped her tears.

Tonya shook her head. "No."

Before Tonya, Le Ly, and Maria could transfer their energy and care to Whitney, the bell rang, calling the class in for the second half of the day.

Whitney could barely make it through the rest of the day without bursting into tears. She was humiliated and embarrassed. "What could she have possibly done to upset Kim and the clique?" she asked herself the entire day, without reaching a conclusion.

Today more than any other day, Whitney was relieved to hear the dismissal bell. She ran for the classroom door as if she were about to score the winning point in a soccer championship. As she approached the front door of the school, she could see out of the side of her eye that Tonya, Le Ly, and Maria were running after her. However, with no goalies to guard the door, she wasn't about to turn back. She was home free and homebound.

Finally, she could burst into tears. And that is what she did the entire way home.

Whitney's thoughts whirled around inside her like a tornado, picking up things as it goes along and tossing them about until everything is in disorder. There was a mess in her mind. She didn't know what to think, what to feel, or what to do.

The ten-year-old wished more than anything that her Nana was still around. Nana would know exactly what to tell her. She would make things better again.

Still sobbing, Whitney opened the door of her home and looked at once for Bailey. She was crying so hard that she could barely call for him.

But he knew to come immediately to her, as he always did when she got home from school.

"Oh, Bailey, I'm so upset." She hugged him, and wiped her tears with his fur.

Before Whitney even thought of the Emerald Bible, Bailey was guiding her down the stairs to the basement. He hopped on Nana's favorite chair and barked.

"You know exactly what I should do, don't you, Bailey!" Whitney guessed that Nana was somehow with them, suggesting that she read from the special Bible.

"Okay, Bailey, you're right. Let's read a story from Nana's Bible."

Before opening the Bible, Whitney remembered the words that Nana spoke to her just before dying: "Whatever you do in the years ahead, keep this Bible with you, as it will help you with all of life's most difficult lessons. And remember, when you open its pages, I am there with you."

Whitney held the precious gift Nana had given her. A smile glossed over her wet face. She took a deep breath, preparing herself for the adventurous world that the Bible had taken her to before. Finally, she looked up to heaven and said, "Nana, read me a story this afternoon. Choose a story of wisdom for me."

Rays of light emerged as Whitney gently opened the emerald cover. She thumbed through its delicate pages until her eyes stopped at a certain paragraph. She began to read aloud . . .

"When Israel went to battle against the Philistines, the two armies stood facing each other. The Philistines stood on the mountain on one side, and the Israelites stood on the mountain on the other side. A great valley lay between them."

CHAPTER TWO

ISRAEL GOES TO WAR

As soon as Whitney looked up from reading the paragraph, she found herself in a setting similar to the one in which she met Joseph and his brothers. There were tents all around, and there were people dressed in robes. Whitney guessed that the people were shepherds, just as Jacob and his sons were.

Everyone was scurrying about. It looked as if they were preparing for something important. "I wonder what in the world is going on here," Whitney thought to herself.

A handsome boy about Whitney's age introduced himself.

"Hi, I'm David, son of Jesse. Who are you?"

"I'm Whitney," the young girl responded with spunk. "And this here is my pup, Bailey."

"Who is your father?" David inquired.

"Peter Bickham. Why?" Whitney asked, somewhat confused as to why that would be David's second question to her.

"Well, because here we usually introduce ourselves by naming our ancestors. That way you know our family heritage, which is very important to us. Often, when we name our ancestors, we figure out that members of our family were friends or relatives of people we meet."

"Well . . . let's see . . . do you know Nana Bickham?" Whitney asked.

"I don't know. Who is she the daughter of?" David questioned.

"Let's see, that would be my great

grandpa, who is Charles Bickham. Do you know him?"

"Hmm . . . no, to be honest with you, I can't say that I do," David admitted.

"Oh well, she was a wonderful grandma, and I miss her a lot," Whitney told David.

"What land are you from?" David asked, now even more curious about the girl in front of him who had seemed to appear out of nowhere.

"Chicago," Whitney responded. She halfway expected him not to know where this was. Jacob, Joseph, and Jonah hadn't, and they were pretty smart.

"I'm sorry to say that I don't know that land," David replied honestly.

"Where exactly are we right now?" Whitney asked David, trusting that he would be a little gentler than the sailors on Jonah's ship in explaining the whereabouts of Bailey and herself.

"Let's see," David began to explain. "Do you know the land of Canaan?"

"Yep, I do," Whitney proudly responded, recalling the story of Joseph and his brothers. "It is by the Great Sea," she continued, showing off her knowledge of the geography of the Middle East. After each story Whitney read, she would go back and look up where she had been on the map of present-day Israel. She found that the names of the cities and seas fit with a map of Israel way back before the birth of Christ. By looking up where she had been and

Great
Sea

Sea
of
Galilee

Dead
Sea

comparing the present-day map with the ancient one, she knew more and more about this land each time she entered it.

"Well, we are close to the city of Jerusalem, in the town of Bethlehem."

"We are in Bethlehem!" Whitney exclaimed with enthusiasm, remembering back to the nativity story. She had always dreamed of going to Bethlehem to visit the place where Jesus was born.

"Yes, why should that excite you?" David asked.

"Ummm . . . ," Whitney thought for a minute. She had to get her time line in order. She remembered that the world of David existed before the birth of Christ. She didn't want to confuse David, so she didn't say anything about Baby Jesus being born in Bethlehem.

"I just like the name," she explained.

Now that she had a better idea of her whereabouts, Whitney wanted to know why everyone seemed so busy. In the story of Jonah and that of Joseph, the people were much more relaxed than those in this town.

"OK, now that I know where we are, can you tell me why everyone here is so panicky? Are they getting ready for an important event or something?" Whitney asked David.

"Well, sort of," David tried to explain.

"See, Israel is at war with the Philistines. We are all a little nervous because the Philistines have a very strong army and lots of armor. Many of us are running back and forth between Bethlehem and the valley of Elah, where our men have set up camp. Not only do we have to worry about feeding the flocks here in Bethlehem, but we need to take care of our men on the front lines of battle, providing them with food and supplies. It is a very busy time."

"Oh, I see. That's kind of scary," Whitney said, hoping she and Bailey would be safe in this land with a war going on.

David continued explaining his situation. "In fact, right now I am preparing to go up to the camp to check on my brothers. My father has asked me to take grain and cheese to the army and to bring home news of them.

"My three older brothers went to battle. I'm a little worried about them, and I know my father is, too. I try to go to the camp when I can get someone here to watch the sheep for me."

Whitney felt comfortable with David and didn't want to see him go. She hadn't met anyone else in Bethlehem. She hadn't even been introduced to Jesse, David's father. She wanted to tag along with David and make the trip to the valley of Elah. However, she was hesitant because she knew a war was going on there, and that was very scary. Before she had decided whether to say anything to David, he invited her to go with him.

"Why don't you and your pup come with me?" David asked.

Whitney was flattered by his invitation, especially since she hadn't had too many invitations in the last couple of weeks. She was hoping he would invite her. Without thinking too much about it, she accepted.

"Sure, why not? Right, Bailey? Let's go."

Bailey barked with enthusiasm. He was excited for the trip. Unlike Chicago, where he was confined to a small area of grass, he could run about freely here. He loved the arid climate and the different kinds of vegetation around him. In fact, Bailey loved entering this world of adventure just as much as Whitney did.

CHAPTER THREE

THE VALLEY OF ELAH

Whitney and Bailey stayed with David in Bethlehem for the night. The three rose early the next morning and headed toward the valley of Elah.

"You will soon see that the battle line is very interesting. The Philistines stand on one mountain. They have set up their camp in a place called Ephes-dammim, between the towns of Socoh and Azekah. The Israelite army has set up camp on the mountain on the other side. There is a large valley between the two camps."

David, Whitney, and Bailey reached the valley of Elah just as the

army was going forth to the battle line.

"Israel is the true nation!" the army shouted, approaching the Philistines. "Our God is with us!"

The three travelers could hear the echo of the battle cry as they approached the camp.

"Hurry, Whitney!" David said anxiously, starting to run. "We must follow the army to the battle line!"

"But, David . . . is that safe?" Whitney asked, a little nervous about running toward the ranks. There was no time to think. Whitney and Bailey were at the mercy of David in this new land.

Sprinting forward, David dropped off the food that Jesse had given him with the keeper at the camp and continued forth to the front line of battle, where his brothers were. Dragging a little behind were Whitney and Bailey. Although Whitney was a fast runner and outpaced everyone on her soccer team, she couldn't keep up with

David. He was so quick that Whitney
and Bailey almost lost sight of him.

"David! Get back! What are you
doing here?" David's eldest brother,
Eliab, said to him, surprised to see his
little brother running toward the
battlefield.

"Return to the camp at once! It is
not safe for
you here!"
Shammah, his
other brother, added.

"But . . . ," David
interrupted them. "I am
supposed to take
home news of you to
father."

Just then
Whitney and Bailey
reached the place of
battle. Trying to catch her
breath, Whitney began to look for

David. He was easy to spot because he was the smallest boy among all the men.

"There he is! Over there, Bailey!" Whitney shouted, not caring if anyone else heard her.

As Whitney and her pup ran toward David and his brothers, the men stopped shouting their war cry and grew very quiet. The army huddled together, like a football team discussing their next move. Whitney wondered what was going on. She and Bailey ran like mad to meet David and his brothers.

CHAPTER FOUR

DAVID CHALLENGES GOLIATH

A deep, strong voice echoed throughout the valley: "I have come here every morning asking you for a warrior with whom I can fight. And still you do not send out someone to meet me. Are you not the army of Israel who wish to fight us Philistines?

"Choose a man for yourselves and let him come down to me. If he is able to fight with me and kill me, then the Philistines will be your servants; but if I prevail against him and kill him, then Israel shall be our servants and serve us."

Whitney looked down into the valley to see who was speaking. At once she realized why the men of Israel crowded together as though they were stuck to one another with super glue. This Philistine warrior was humongous in size. He was a true giant, like Paul Bunyan with Babe the blue ox, or the giant in the story of Jack and the beanstalk.

At first Whitney thought he might not be real. "Perhaps two people have fit inside a Halloween costume. Or maybe it is a man wearing stilts," she guessed. There had to be an explanation for his enormous proportions.

Not only was he tall and wide, but he was covered in armor. He wore a helmet of bronze on his head and was armed with a coat of mail that weighed at least 150 pounds. There was more bronze on his legs and between his shoulders. And the shaft of his spear

was like a weaver's beam, the head of
it weighing at least twenty pounds.
He carried with him a shield, the
length of which was taller than
Whitney.

Whitney and everyone at the
camp were amazed at the giant's size
and strength, and, needless to say,
terribly frightened by him. The giant
was not only physically intimidating,
but also he was angry. The tone of
his voice alone would scare off
anyone.

"Who is that guy?" David asked
one of the men.

"His name is Goliath. Goliath of
Gath," the man replied. "He is the
champion, the largest and strongest
warrior of the Philistines."

David looked around for Saul,
who was at that time the king of
Israel.

"Surely Saul has designated

someone to fight this giant. Who is the
brave man?" David was curious.

But no one came forward.

David continued his questioning.
"What will the reward be for the person
who fights the giant and kills him?"

Eliab, the eldest brother, was
angry upon hearing David's questions.
He turned to him with wrath and said,
"David, why have you come here? Were
you merely curious about the war?

"Who is tending father's sheep?"
Eliab asked his younger brother. "You
need to return home to your
responsibilities. Your job here is
finished."

David rebuked, "Why are you
angry with me? What have I done to
you? I have come here to bring you
food and supplies and to get news to
bring home to father." David wanted to
stop at this, but he couldn't resist telling
everyone how he felt about the giant.

"But I can't believe no one in this

army is going to stand up to this bully. After all, we have God on our side, who will fight for us. Goliath has no God with him." David paused, and then said something Whitney was sure he would regret.

"I will fight the giant. I am not afraid of him."

As soon as he spoke these words, David was surrounded by madness. The bewildered men turned to each other to make sure they weren't mistaken in what they had just heard.

Amid the chaos, Whitney seized the opportunity to tap David on the back.

"Are you crazy?! Why did you just say that? You aren't actually going to fight that superhuman or whatever he is, are you? Think about it . . . he will smash you!"

"I know what I am doing," he replied with confidence.

"But David . . . ," Whitney pressed on. Before she could finish her question, David was taken to Saul, who had personally sent for the boy.

"What is this I hear you say?" Saul asked David. "Do you know what you are saying, boy? Look at this man. He is at least four times your size, and has been a warrior since his youth."

David knew all this to be true, but it did not mean anything to him. "I understand," he responded to the king, "but the same Lord who has many times saved me from the paw of the lion and from the paw of the bear as I shepherd my father's flock will also save me from the hand of Goliath. The Lord is with Israel and will defend us."

Saul was amazed at the young boy's faith and sent him out to fight the giant.

CHAPTER FIVE

THE SECRET WEAPON

Whitney and Bailey made their way over to Saul, who at this point was giving David his official blessing.

"Go, and may the Lord be with you!" the king said as he laid his right hand on the forehead of David.

As Whitney approached, Saul was dressing David in armor. He put a bronze helmet on his head and clothed him with a coat of mail. Saul strapped his own sword over David's armor.

David walked five steps forward and returned.

"Saul, I cannot wear this armor. I'm not used to it, and I feel clumsy. It

is better for me to be free and nimble."

Whitney was relieved to see David return to Saul. It was her last chance to talk some sense into him.

"David . . . hold on . . . wait!" Whitney yelled to him as he took off again to meet the giant.

"Whitney, I'm sorry . . . but I have to do this," David explained to his friend with a determination that Whitney had never seen in anyone before. "I must do it for my nation, for my family, and for myself. But most importantly, I must do it for my God. The Lord is with us, and if I don't fight and kill this giant, then everyone will doubt the Lord's power. You and everyone else must have faith in me and in the living God who is with our people."

Whitney looked at David and could not say a thing. As she stared into his eyes, she began to understand where his courage and strength were coming from.

"You really do think you will be OK, don't you?" Whitney asked.

David nodded.

She thought briefly about her own situation at school and wished she had some of David's faith. With courage like his, she could face Kim and the popular group at school instead of running away from them.

"After all," she thought, "crying to myself is not going to do me any good. And Tonya, Maria, and Le Ly are so intimidated by Kim, Nicki, and Mary Jo that I know I can't count on their help."

Whitney had taken a second too long to ponder these things. By the time she tuned into David again, he had already started walking toward Goliath.

"David! One more thing!" Whitney shouted. The young girl bent down to the ground and searched for some strings and animal hide that would work as a sling, and some small rocks. Her brother had taught her how to make a sling and use it to hurl a stone.

The boy returned, but was anxious to get his battle over with.

"Here," Whitney said, handing him a newly made sling and five smooth stones.

"These are to help you with your

battle. They are small enough for you to carry without feeling heavy, as you did with the armor. And if you use them correctly, they can be quite powerful."

"How do they work?" David asked, somewhat confused by the looks of them.

"It's easy," Whitney explained. "You use the sling to launch the stones."

"Oh, I see. That's neat," David said, pleased with his new toy. "Where did you learn this trick?"

"My brother taught it to me. He is always getting into trouble," Whitney said. "Now, go on your way. I trust that you will come back safely to us."

CHAPTER SIX

TRIUMPH OVER THE GIANT

As soon as David met Goliath, the giant began to roar with laughter. He was so big that when he laughed, the earth beneath him shook.

"This is who you have given me to fight?" Goliath mocked David. "A boy? Better yet, the smallest among you?"

His laughter turned into wrath, and he shouted, "Is this some kind of joke?"

Goliath then directed his attention to David and said, "Am I a dog, that you come after me with string?" Goliath eyed the sling in David's hand.

"Fine then," he continued, "I will feed your flesh to the birds of the air and to the wild animals of the field."

The giant cursed David by his gods.

But David was not afraid. He walked toward the Philistine, saying, "You come to me with a sword and a spear, but I come to you in the name of the Lord. The God of the armies of Israel will strike you down and deliver you into my hand. And I will give the dead bodies of the Philistine army to the birds of the air and to the wild animals of the earth, so that all the earth may know that there is a God in Israel.

David had not even finished speaking when Goliath charged after him. Before the giant had reached the boy, David quickly took one of the stones that Whitney had given him and skillfully used the sling to hurl it at the giant.

The stone flew across the field like an arrow to its target. It hit the giant directly on the forehead, and Goliath fell to the ground like a tree that had been hit by lightning. David immediately ran over to him, grabbed his sword, and killed him.

Everyone around Whitney shouted with triumph. Saul and his army could not believe what had just happened before their eyes. Even Bailey was jumping up and down with excitement.

Whitney and Bailey ran to meet David. They were the first to hug and kiss David and congratulate him on his victory.

David turned to Whitney and said, "Did I not tell you that the Lord would protect me and deliver the giant into my hands?"

"David, you have helped me to believe," she confessed with sincerity.

"Will you and Bailey come home to Bethlehem with me and my brothers to share in the celebration?" David asked.

"We'd love to!" Whitney automatically replied, delighted that she had been invited to a party. In the excitement and joy of David's victory, she had forgotten about her own battle

in Chicago. She became anxious to resolve it.

"You know what, David? I have my own battle to fight back home. I'd better go to it while I still have some of your faith."

"I understand," David said, a little disappointed that Whitney and her pup would not be there to celebrate with him. After all, it was Whitney who had taught him how to use the sling.

"Whitney, thank you for everything, especially for the sling and the stones," David said as he bid farewell to his newfound friend.

Looking into her eyes, David recognized in Whitney the same strength and determination that helped him tackle the giant. "You have the faith and courage inside of you, too, Whitney. Remember that when you fight your battle."

With tears beginning to form in her eyes, she responded, "I will."

David knelt down to pet Bailey one last time. He would surely miss this pup, who had become as much his buddy as Whitney.

Whitney was relieved to find that her Emerald Bible was still with her. She was afraid she had left it back in Bethlehem.

With a renewed conviction to face Kim and the mess she left behind in Chicago, Whitney opened the book to the last paragraph of the story of David and Goliath. She began to read:

"On David's return from killing the Philistine, Abner, the commander of the Israelite army, took David and brought him before Saul. Saul asked the boy, 'Whose son are you, young man?' And David answered, 'I am the son of your servant Jesse the Bethlehemite.'"

CHAPTER SEVEN

WHITNEY AND HER GIANT

As soon as Whitney looked up from reading the last word in the paragraph, she found herself once again seated on Nana's favorite chair, with Bailey secure in her lap.

Her wet face of tears had dried, and she sat quietly on the chair, remembering the lesson that she had learned from David.

She looked up to heaven and thanked Nana for the great story. And she asked Nana to be with her as she confronted her own giant.

"Nana, grant me the courage to stand up for myself. And help me to always believe in myself and in God," Whitney prayed.

Whitney knew exactly what she needed to do.

"I will call Kim at home and ask her what I have done to upset her. I am going to tell her that I think it is unfair the way she is excluding me."

But this was easier said than done. Like Tonya, Maria, and Le Ly, Whitney was intimidated by Kim and the group. And she had more reason to be than the others. After all, she was the new kid on the block, trying to fit in. Tonya, Maria, and Le Ly at least had themselves. Whitney felt alone in her battle against the clique.

"I must remember what David told me," she reminded herself. His words came back to her and echoed through her mind: "You have the faith and courage inside of you."

She repeated this to herself three

times before picking up the phone to call Kim.

Whitney's stomach churned as the phone on the other end rang. On the third ring, someone picked up.

"Hello."

"Uh . . . hi. Is Kim home?" Whitney asked, barely able to utter these words.

"Yeah, hang on." It sounded like Kim's little sister.

"Kim! Kim! Someone is on the phone for you," the girl yelled.

And then there was silence.

The pause seemed like an eternity to Whitney. She wanted so badly to hang up the phone before Kim answered. But she repeated David's words to herself over and over again until Kim finally picked up the phone.

"Hello," Whitney heard from the other end of the phone.

"Uhh . . . uhh . . . ," Whitney

stuttered. She completely blanked out. The speech that she had rehearsed perfectly just minutes before was useless. Not only did she forget what to say, but she forgot why she was calling.

"I must be going mad," she thought to herself.

"Hello?" Kim said again.

"Yeah . . . hi Kim. It's Whitney," she finally responded.

"Uh . . . ." Now it was Kim's time to stutter. She was taken completely off guard, just as Goliath was when he saw a little boy coming after him with a stick.

Kim didn't know what to say. She couldn't make small talk. She knew that Whitney had heard the hurtful things she said about her to Tonya. And she didn't have the other girls on the phone to support her. Without Nicki and Mary Jo by her side, Kim felt powerless.

"Yes, Whitney. What do you want?" Kim asked.

"Better to just get to the point and get this conversation over with," Kim thought to herself.

"Well . . . ," Whitney paused again. The rehearsed speech came back to her, and she remembered why she was calling.

"Well, I wanted to tell you that I am very hurt by your excluding me from your party."

"Whew! That felt good," Whitney said to herself, gaining a little more confidence. She figured she had better continue while she was still feeling good.

"I have not done anything intentionally to hurt you. Yet you act against me as though I have."

There it was. It was out. Whitney had just laid her hurt feelings on the table. Now it was Kim's turn.

The brave girl felt as though she was standing in the valley of Elah with

74

David and had just taken her first strike at the giant. She was now on the defensive, waiting to see what the giant would do.

She prepared herself for the worst—to hear the many reasons Kim had for not inviting her. But instead there was just silence. And more silence.

"Well, to be honest Whitney, I feel like you are too friendly with Mike and Joe. They were my friends first, and I feel like you are stealing them away," Kim began to explain with a hint of jealousy in her voice.

"Wait a minute," Whitney interrupted. "I have no intention of stealing them away from you and your friends. I figured by getting to know them I would be more accepted by your group. And I merely enjoy playing soccer with them. Nothing else."

"Oh," Kim responded, relieved to

know that Whitney wasn't out to steal the popular boys from her and her friends. "OK . . . well, I understand that a little better now."

Both girls stopped talking for a moment. Then Kim broke the awkward silence.

"Whitney, when I first moved to Chicago two years ago, I had to do a lot of proving of myself to others. People gave me a really hard time at first. You've been accepted so easily by everyone. Frankly, it seems unfair. I guess part of me wanted to give you a taste of what I went through."

Whitney was glad to know that she wasn't the only one who had not been born and raised in Chicago. It seemed as

though everyone at her school had known each other their entire lives. And she appreciated Kim's honesty.

"Kim," Whitney chimed in, "I have had my share of proving myself to people, too. It has not been that easy for me."

"Yeah, I guess you're right. I don't know what all you've been through to get here," Kim said with sincerity. She was sorry that she had made life more difficult for Whitney. Whitney could hear remorse in her voice.

"I'll tell you what," Kim continued, in a cheerful tone. "From this point on, I will make your life easier.

"And by the way, would you like to come to my party tomorrow night?"

"I'd love to!" Whitney exclaimed, with more enthusiasm than any other person on Kim's guest list.

Whitney hung up the phone. It was time for her own celebration. She had learned from David a lesson that she would carry with her for the rest of her life.

THE EMERALD BIBLE
COLLECTION

Also in
THE EMERALD BIBLE COLLECTION

WHITNEY RIDES THE WHALE
WITH JONAH
and learns she can't run away

WHITNEY SEWS JOSEPH'S
MANY-COLORED COAT
and learns a lesson about jealousy

WHITNEY SOLVES A DILEMMA
WITH SOLOMON
and learns the importance of honesty

ABOUT THE AUTHOR

Therese Johnson Borchard has always been inspired by the wisdom of the Bible's stories. As a young child, especially, she was intrigued by biblical characters and awed by their courage. She pursued her interest in religion and obtained a B.A. in religious studies from Saint Mary's College, Notre Dame, and an M.A. in theology from the University of Notre Dame. She has published various books and pamphlets in which she creatively retells the great stories of the Judeo-Christian tradition.

ABOUT THE ILLUSTRATOR

Wendy VanNest began drawing as a small, fidgety child seated beside her father at church. He gave her his bulletin to scribble on to help her keep still during the service. People around them began donating their bulletins, asking her for artwork, and at the end of the service, an usher would always give her his carnation boutonniere. As a result of this early encouragement, she pursued her interest and passion in art, and has been drawing ever since.